Pig
AND
o
small

by Alex Latimer

PEACHTREE
ATLANTA

for Sophie, Lily & Olivia

Published by
PEACHTREE PUBLISHERS
1700 Chattahoochee Avenue
Atlanta, Georgia 30318-2112
www.peachtree-online.com

Originally published in Great Britain in 2013 by Picture Corgi,
an imprint of Random House Children's Books
First United States edition published in 2014 by Peachtree Publishers

Illustrations created as pencil drawings, digitized, then finished
with color and texture

Printed in April 2014 in China by Toppen Leefung

10 9 8 7 6 5 4 3 2 1
First edition

Library of Congress Cataloging-in-Publication Data

Latimer, Alex, author, illustrator.
Pig and small / by Alex Latimer.
    pages cm
ISBN: 978-1-56145-797-7
Summary: Their size difference proves to be an obstacle to becoming
friends until Pig and Bug find something they both enjoy doing.
[1. Size—Fiction. 2. Friendship—Fiction. 3. Pigs—Fiction. 4. Insects—Fiction.] I. Title.
PZ7.L369612Pi 2014
[E]—dc23
                                    2013045423

Before this morning, Pig's nose had never squeaked—not even once.

But since this morning, all it ever did was squeak.

It squeaked during breakfast.

It squeaked while he was feeding pigeons in the park.

And it squeaked nonstop in the bath.

So Pig got the big medical book down from his bookshelf, and looked up Squeaky Nose Syndrome.

But there was nothing in the book about it.

Pig touched his nose—
it felt normal.

Then he breathed in
through his nostrils.
They worked fine.

Finally he squinted
and peered down
his snout.

There, standing on the end of his nose, was a tiny bug, and it was waving and squeaking like crazy!

"Hello," said Pig.
"Squeak, squeak," replied Bug.

Pig could tell by the way the bug was waving
and squeaking that it wanted to be friends.

So Pig got his tandem
bicycle out of the shed . . .

and Pig and Bug rode down
to the park together.

Pig couldn't help feeling
as though he'd done most
of the pedaling.

To make up for Pig having to do all the work, Bug gave Pig a delicious cake he'd baked that very morning.

Pig just ate the whole thing in one
bite without appreciating the way Bug
had decorated it.

"How about a game of chess
to cheer you up?" asked Pig.

By the time Bug had made the first move . . .

Pig was fast asleep.

When Pig woke up, Bug had knitted a matching pair of sweaters—one for himself and one for Pig.

Although Pig said he liked his new sweater very much, he couldn't fit it over his head.

Pig and Bug were very sad. They'd tried so hard to be friends, but it just wasn't working.

So they said goodbye . . .

and parted ways.

Just then, as Pig was
walking away,
the wind picked up
and blew a newspaper
right into his face.

And this is what Pig saw:

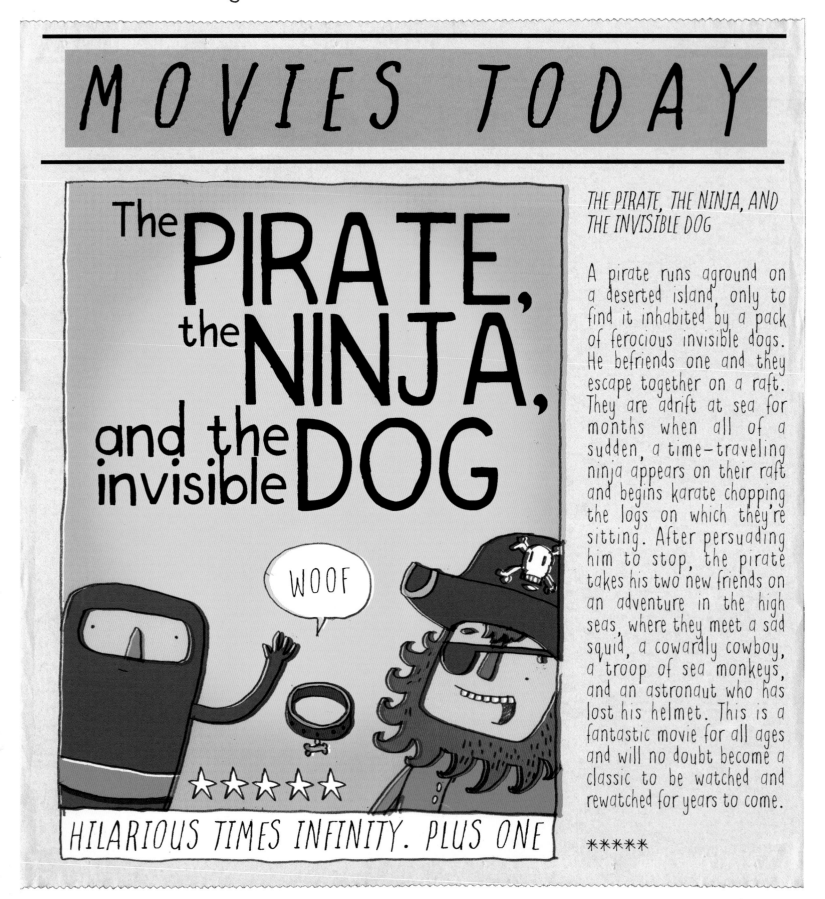

Pig rushed off
to the movies.

BOX OFFICE

"A ticket for one seat please—my friend will sit on my ear. And just one box of popcorn," said Pig.

"Bug doesn't eat much at all."

They were almost late for the start of the show, but Bug helped Pig to find the way to their seat in record time.

Then the movie started.

When Bug got scared, he hid behind Pig's ear.

Aha hah hah ha

And when Pig didn't get a joke, Bug explained it to him.

When the movie was finished, they
walked home and talked all about it.

They were thrilled they had found something that they
both enjoyed doing. It made them think of a few other
things they could do together as friends.

The next day they
visited an art gallery,

the aquarium,

and the theater.